J. R. Ward lives in the South with her incredibly supportive husband and her beloved golden retriever. After graduating from law school, she began working in health care in Boston and spent many years as chief of staff for one of the premier academic medical centres in the nation.

Visit her and the Black Dagger Brotherhood at www.jrward.com

LOVER
AVENGED

J. R. WARD

piatkus

PIATKUS

First published in the United States in 2009 by New American Library,
A Division of Penguin Group (USA) Inc, New York
First published in Great Britain as a paperback original in 2009 by Piatkus
Reprinted 2009, 2010

Copyright © Jessica Bird 2009

The moral right of the author has been asserted.

A CIP catalogue record for this book
is available from the British Library.

ISBN 978-0-7499-4173-4

Typeset in Garamond by Palimpsest Book Production Limited,
Grangemouth, Stirlingshire
Printed in the UK by CPI Mackays, Chatham ME5 8TD

Papers used by Piatkus are natural, renewable and
recyclable products sourced from well-managed forests and certified
in accordance with the rules of the Forest Stewardship Council.

Mixed Sources
Product group from well-managed
forests and other controlled sources
www.fsc.org Cert no. SGS-COC-004081
© 1996 Forest Stewardship Council

Piatkus
An imprint of
Little, Brown Book Group
100 Victoria Embankment
London EC4Y 0DY

An Hachette UK Company
www.hachette.co.uk

www.piatkus.co.uk

DEDICATED TO *YOU*:

Good *and* bad *have never been more relative terms*
than when applied to the likes of you.
But I agree with her. To me, you have always been a hero.

ACKNOWLEDGMENTS

With immense gratitude to the readers of the Black Dagger Brotherhood and a shout-out to the Cellies!

Thank you so very much: Steven Axelrod, Kara Cesare, Claire Zion, Kara Welsh, and Leslie Gelbman.

Thank you, Lu and Opal, as well as our Mods and all our Hall Monitors, for everything you do out of the goodness of your hearts!

As always with many thanks to my Executive Committee: Sue Grafton, Dr. Jessica Andersen, and Betsey Vaughan. And with much respect to the incomparable Suzanne Brockmann and the ever-fabulous Christine Feehan (and family).

To D.L.B.—to say I look up to you would be self-obvious but there you go. Love u xxx mummy

To N.T.M.—who is always right, and still manages to be loved by all of us.

To LeElla Scott—who *owns* it, baby, yeah, she so does.

To Kaylie-girl and her momma—'cuz I love them so.

None of this would be possible without: my loving husband, who is my adviser and caretaker and visionary; my wonderful mother, who has given me so much love I couldn't possibly ever repay her; my family (both those of blood and those by adoption); and my dearest friends.

Oh, and with love to the better half of WriterDog, as always.

GLOSSARY OF TERMS
AND PROPER NOUNS

ahstrux nohstrum (n.) Private guard with license to kill who is granted his or her position by the king.

ahvenge (v.) Act of mortal retribution, typically carried out by a male loved one.

Black Dagger Brotherhood (pr. n.) Highly trained vampire warriors who protect their species against the Lessening Society. As a result of selective breeding within the race, Brothers possess immense physical and mental strength, as well as rapid healing capabilities. They are not siblings, for the most part, and are inducted into the Brotherhood upon nomination by the Brothers. Aggressive, self-reliant, and secretive by nature, they exist apart from civilians, having little contact with members of the other classes except when they need to feed. They are the subjects of legend and the objects of reverence within the vampire world. They may be killed by only the most serious of wounds, e.g., a gunshot or stab to the heart, etc.

blood slave (n.) Male or female vampire who has been subjugated to serve the blood needs of another. The practice of keeping blood slaves has recently been outlawed.

chrih (n.) Symbol of honorable death in the Old Language.

the Chosen (n.) Female vampires who have been bred to serve the Scribe Virgin. They are considered members of the aristocracy, though they are spiritually rather than temporally focused. They have little or no interaction with males other than the Primale, but can be mated to Brothers at the Scribe Virgin's direction to further propagate their class. Some have the ability to prognosticate. In the past, they were used to meet the blood needs of unmated members of the Brotherhood, and that practice has been reinstated by the Brothers.

cohntehst (n.) Conflict between two males competing for the right to be a female's mate.

doggen (n.) Member of the servant class within the vampire world. *Doggen* have old, conservative traditions about service to their superiors and follow a formal code of dress and behavior. They are able to go out during the day, but they age relatively quickly. Life expectancy is approximately five hundred years.

Dhunhd (pr. n.) Hell.

ehros (n.) A Chosen trained in the matter of sexual arts.

exhile dhoble (n.) The evil or cursed twin, the one born second.

the Fade (pr. n.) Nontemporal realm where the dead reunite with their loved ones and pass eternity.

First Family (pr. n.) The king and queen of the vampires, and any children they may have.

ghardian (n.) Custodian of an individual. There are varying degrees of *ghardians*, with the most powerful being that of a *sehcluded* female.

glymera (n.) The social core of the aristocracy, roughly equivalent to Regency England's ton.

granhmen (n.) Grandmother.

hellren (n.) Male vampire who has been mated to a female. Males may take more than one female as mate.

leahdyre (n.) A person of power and influence.

leelan (adj.) A term of endearment loosely translated as "dearest one."

Lessening Society (pr. n.) Order of slayers convened by the Omega for the purpose of eradicating the vampire species.

lesser (n.) De-souled human who targets vampires for extermination as a member of the Lessening Society. *Lessers* must be stabbed through the chest in order to be killed; otherwise they are ageless. They do not eat or drink and are impotent. Over time, their hair, skin, and irises lose pigmentation until they are blond, blushless, and pale eyed. They smell like baby powder. Inducted into the society by the Omega, they retain a ceramic jar thereafter into which their heart was placed after it was removed.

lewlhen (n.) Gift.

lheage (n.) A term of respect used by a sexual submissive to refer to her dominant.

lys (n.) Torture tool used to remove the eyes.

mahmen (n.) Mother. Used both as an identifier and a term of affection.

mhis (n.) The masking of a given physical environment; the creation of a field of illusion.

nalla (n. f.) or *nallum* (n. m.) Beloved.

needing period (n.) Female vampire's time of fertility, generally lasting for two days and accompanied by intense sexual cravings. Occurs approximately five years after a female's transition and then once a decade thereafter. All males respond to some degree if they are around a female in her need. It can be a dangerous time, with conflicts and fights breaking out between competing males, particularly if the female is not mated.

newling (n.) A virgin.

the Omega (pr. n.) Malevolent, mystical figure who has targeted the vampires for extinction out of resentment directed toward the Scribe Virgin. Exists in a non-temporal realm and has extensive powers, though not the power of creation.

pherarsom (adj.) Term referring to the potency of a male's sexual organs. Literal translation something close to "worthy of entering a female."

princeps (n.) Highest level of the vampire aristocracy, second only to members of the First Family or the

Scribe Virgin's Chosen. Must be born to the title; it may not be conferred.

pyrocant (n.) Refers to a critical weakness in an individual. The weakness can be internal, such as an addiction, or external, such as a lover.

rahlman (n.) Savior.

rythe (n.) Ritual manner of assuaging honor granted by one who has offended another. If accepted, the offended chooses a weapon and strikes the offender, who presents him- or herself without defenses.

the Scribe Virgin (pr. n.) Mystical force who is counselor to the king as well as the keeper of vampire archives and the dispenser of privileges. Exists in a nontemporal realm and has extensive powers. Capable of a single act of creation, which she expended to bring the vampires into existence.

sehclusion (n.) Status conferred by the king upon a female of the aristocracy as a result of a petition by the female's family. Places the female under the sole direction of her *ghardian*, typically the eldest male in her household. Her *ghardian* then has the legal right to determine all manner of her life, restricting at will any and all interactions she has with the world.

shellan (n.) Female vampire who has been mated to a male. Females generally do not take more than one mate due to the highly territorial nature of bonded males.

symphath (n.) Subspecies within the vampire race characterized by the ability and desire to manipulate emotions in others (for the purposes of an energy exchange), among other traits. Historically, they have been discriminated against and, during certain eras, hunted by vampires. They are near to extinction.

the Tomb (pr. n.) Sacred vault of the Black Dagger Brotherhood. Used as a ceremonial site as well as a storage facility for the jars of *lessers*. Ceremonies performed there include inductions, funerals, and disciplinary actions against Brothers. No one may enter except for members of the Brotherhood, the Scribe Virgin, or candidates for induction.

trahyner (n.) Word used between males of mutual respect and affection. Translated loosely as "beloved friend."

transition (n.) Critical moment in a vampire's life when he or she transforms into an adult. Thereafter, they must drink the blood of the opposite sex to survive and are unable to withstand sunlight. Occurs generally in the mid-twenties. Some vampires do not live through their transitions, males in particular. Prior to their transitions, vampires are physically weak, sexually unaware and unresponsive, and unable to dematerialize.

vampire (n.) Member of a species separate from that of Homo sapiens. Vampires must drink the blood of the opposite sex to survive. Human blood will keep them alive, though the strength does not last long. Following their transitions, which occur in their mid-twenties, they are unable to go out into sunlight and must feed from the vein regularly. Vampires cannot "convert" humans through a bite or transfer of blood, though they are in rare cases able to breed with the other species. Vampires can dematerialize at will, though they must be able to calm themselves and concentrate to do so and may not carry anything heavy with them. They are able to strip the memories of humans, provided such memories are short term. Some vampires are able to read minds. Life expectancy is upward of a thousand years, or in some cases even longer.

wahlker (n.) An individual who has died and returned to the living from the Fade. They are accorded great respect and are revered for their travails.

whard (n.) Equivalent of a godfather or godmother to an individual.

All kings are blind.
The good ones see this and use more than their eyes to lead.

ONE

"The king must die."

Four single-syllable words. One by one they were nothing special. Put together? They called up all kinds of bad shit: Murder. Betrayal. Treason.

Death.

In the thick moments after they were spoken to him, Rehvenge kept quiet, letting the quartet hang in the stuffy air of the study, four points of a dark, evil compass he was intimately familiar with.

"Have you any response?" Montrag, son of Rehm, said.

"Nope."

Montrag blinked and fiddled with the silk cravat at his neck. Like most members of the *glymera*, he had both velvet slippers firmly planted in the dry, rarified sand of his class. Which meant he was just plain precious, all the way around. In his smoking jacket and his natty pin-striped slacks and . . . shit, were those actually spats? . . . he was right out of the pages of *Vanity Fair*. Like, a hundred years ago. And in his myriad condescensions and his bright frickin' ideas, he was Kissinger without a president when it came to politics: all analysis, no authority.

Which explained this meeting, didn't it.

"Don't stop now," Rehv said. "You've already jumped off the building. The landing isn't getting any softer."

Montrag frowned. "I fail to view this with your kind of levity."

"Who's laughing."

A knock on the study's door brought Montrag's head to the side, and he had a profile like an Irish setter: all nose. "Come in."

The *doggen* who followed the command struggled under the weight of the silver service she carried. With an ebony tray the size of a porch in her hands, she humped the load across the room.

Until her head came up and she saw Rehv.

She froze like a snapshot.

"We take our tea here." Montrag pointed to the low-slung table between the two silk sofas they were sitting on. *"Here."*

The *doggen* didn't move, just stared at Rehv's face.

"What *is* the matter?" Montrag demanded as the teacups began to tremble, a chiming noise rising up from the tray. "Place our tea here, now."

The *doggen* bowed her head, mumbled something, and came forward slowly, putting one foot in front of the other like she was approaching a coiled snake. She stayed as far away from Rehv as she could, and after she put the service down, her shaking hands were barely able to get the cups into the saucers.

When she went for the pot of tea, it was clear she was going to spill the shit all over the place.

"Let me do it," Rehv said, reaching out.

As the *doggen* jerked away from him, her grip slipped off the pot handle and the tea went into free fall.

Rehv caught the blistering-hot silver in his palms.

"What have you done!" Montrag said, leaping off of his sofa.

The *doggen* cringed away, her hands going to her face. "I am sorry, master. Verily, I am—"

"Oh, shut up, and get us some ice—"

"It's not her fault." Rehv calmly switched his hold to the handle and poured. "And I'm perfectly fine."

They both stared at him like they were waiting for him to hop up and shake his bumper to the tune of *ow-ow-ow*.

He put the silver pot down and looked into Montrag's pale eyes. "One lump. Or two?"

"May I . . . may I get you something for that burn?"

He smiled, flashing his fangs at his host. "I'm perfectly fine."

Montrag seemed offended that he couldn't do anything, and turned his dissatisfaction on his servant. "You are a total disgrace. Leave us."

Rehv glanced at the *doggen*. To him, her emotions were a three-dimensional grid of fear and shame and panic, the interlocking weave filling out the space around her as surely as her bones and muscles and skin did.

Be of ease, he thought at her. *And know I'll make this right.*

Surprise flared in her face, but the tension left her shoulders and she turned away, looking much calmer.

When she was gone, Montrag cleared his throat and sat back down. "I don't think she's going to work out. She's utterly incompetent."

"Why don't we start with one lump." Rehv dropped a sugar cube into the tea. "And see if you want another."

He held the cup out, but not too far out, so that Montrag was forced to get up again from his sofa and bend across the table.

"Thank you."

Rehv didn't let go of the saucer as he pushed a change of thought into his host's brain. "I make females nervous. It wasn't her fault."

He released his hold abruptly and Montrag scrambled to keep hold of the Royal Doulton.

"Oops. Don't spill." Rehv settled back onto his sofa "Shame to get a stain on this fine rug of yours. Aubusson, is it?"

"Ah . . . yes." Montrag parked it again and frowned, like he had no idea why he felt differently about his maid. "Er . . . yes, it is. My father bought it many years ago. He had exquisite taste, didn't he? We built this room for it because it is so very large, and the color of the walls was chosen specifically to bring out the peach tones."

Montrag looked around the study and smiled to himself as he sipped, his pinkie out in the breeze like a flag.

"How's your tea?"

"Perfect, but won't you have some?"

"Not a tea drinker." Rehv waited until the cup was up to the male's lips. "So you were talking about murdering Wrath?"

Montrag sputtered, Earl Grey dappling the front of his bloodred smoking jacket and hitting Daddy's peachy-keen rug.

As the male batted at the stains with a limp hand, Rehv held out a napkin. "Here, use this."

Montrag took the damask square, awkwardly patted at his chest, then swiped the rug with equal lack of effect. Clearly, he was the kind of male who made messes, not cleaned them up.

"You were saying," Rehv murmured.

Montrag ditched the napkin on the tray and got to his feet, leaving his tea behind as he paced around. He stopped in front of a large mountain landscape and seemed to admire the dramatic scene with its spotlit colonial soldier praying to the heavens.

He spoke to the painting. "You are aware that so many of our blooded brethren have been taken down in the raids by the *lessers*."

"And here I thought I'd been made *leahdyre* of the council just because of my sparkling personality."

Montrag glared over his shoulder, his chin cocked in classic aristocratic fashion. "I lost my father and my mother and all of my first cousins. I buried each one of them. Think you that is a joy?"

"My apologies." Rehv put his right palm over his heart and bowed his head, even though he didn't give a shit. He was not going to be manipulated by the recitation of losses. Especially when the guy's emotions were all about greed, not grief.